"Why can't everyone wear whatever they want to school?" Posey said bravely.

Miss Lee stood up. She squeezed her lips together and thought.

"Well, I guess because then we'd have pirat and clowns and super-heroes a allet dancers in our class," she said last.

"What's wrong with that?" said Posey.

"That doesn't sound very much like a first-grade class, does it?" said Miss Lee.

"No," said Posey. "It sounds like a parade."

PRINCESS P🌼SEY

and the

FIRST GRADE PARADE

PRINCESS POSEY

and the

FIRST GRADE PARADE

Stephanie Greene

ILLUSTRATED BY

Stephanie Roth Sisson

SCHOLASTIC INC.
New York Toronto London Auckland
Sydney Mexico City New Delhi Hong Kong

No part of this publication may be reproduced, stored in a retrieval system, or transmitted in any form or by any means, electronic, mechanical, photocopying, recording, or otherwise, without written permission of the publisher. For information regarding permission, write to Puffin Books, a division of Penguin Young Readers Group, a member of Penguin Group (USA) Inc., 345 Hudson Street, New York, NY 10014.

ISBN 978-0-545-38933-4

Text copyright © 2010 by Stephanie Greene.
Illustrations copyright © 2010 by Stephanie Roth Sisson.
All rights reserved. Published by Scholastic Inc., 557 Broadway, New York, NY 10012, by arrangement with Puffin Books, a division of Penguin Young Readers Group, a member of Penguin Group (USA) Inc. SCHOLASTIC and associated logos are trademarks and/or registered trademarks of Scholastic Inc.

12 11 10 9 8 7 6 5 4 3 2 1   11 12 13 14 15 16/0

Printed in the U.S.A.   40

First Scholastic printing, September 2011

Decorative graphics by Marikka Tamura
Design by Marikka Tamura
Text set in Stempel Garamond

For Ellie and Natalie —S.G.

For Trammell and Olivia —S.R.S.

CONTENTS

CHAPTER ONE

KISS AND GO LANE

"You're leaving me," said Posey.

"I am not leaving you," said her mom. "I am going to drop you off at the front of the school. Miss Lee will be there to meet you at your classroom door."

"It feels like you're leaving me," said Posey.

"All the first-graders walk to their rooms," her mom said. She slipped a spoonful of green peas into Danny's mouth. "You'll be fine. Eat your lunch now."

Posey didn't feel like eating. She was worried about the first day of school. It was only five days away.

Posey was going to be in first grade.

All summer long, her mom had talked about the fun things Posey was going to do. Like draw. And learn to read. And play games.

But all Posey could
think about was the sign in
front of her school.

It said, Kiss and Go Lane.

It was where Posey had to kiss
her mom good-bye.

And open the car door.

And walk into the school.

All by herself.

"Last year you didn't drop me off," Posey said. "You walked me to my class."

"Last year you were no bigger than a minute." Her mom smiled. "You're a big girl now."

"I don't want to be a big girl."

Posey got off her chair and squatted down. She wrapped her arms around her knees. "See? I'm as small as I was last year."

Danny peered at her over the edge of his high chair and laughed.

CHAPTER TWO

THE
PINK
PRINCESS

"**S**it up and finish your lunch," her mom said patiently.

Posey got back on her chair.

"Why aren't you leaving Danny?" she asked.

"I told you," her mom said. "My new job has day care."

"You *should* leave him." Posey wrinkled her nose. "He smells."

"I think he smells sweet." Her mom buried her nose in Danny's neck. He grabbed her hair.

Posey felt the ends of her mouth turn down. "You love Danny more than me," she said.

"Oh, Posey."

Her mom came around the table. She put her arm around Posey's stiff shoulders. "It's going to be fine, sweetie. You'll see. We'll buy you something new to wear."

"Why can't I wear this?"

Posey pointed to her pink tutu. It had a hole above her belly button. The skirt had a tear on one side.

Posey loved to wear it more than anything. She wore it every day, all summer long.

It made her feel special.

Posey never told anyone, but when she wore her pink tutu, she was Princess Posey, the Pink Princess.

Princess Posey could go anywhere. Do anything.

Even walk into first grade by herself.

"You can wear it when you get home from school," said her mom.

Posey didn't want to wear it *after* school. She wanted to wear it *to* school.

Her mom untied Danny's bib.

"You wait with Danny while I get some towels," she said. "We'll go for a swim."

"It's all your fault," Posey said to Danny with a big frown. "I was the baby till you got here."

Danny smiled and grabbed his toes.

"Mom thinks you're great because you're a baby," Posey said. "But you wait."

She leaned forward until their noses were almost touching. "One day she will leave you the way she's leaving me."

Danny blew a bubble and laughed.

CHAPTER THREE

MONSTER
OF THE
BLUE HALL

After Posey went swimming, she ran to the playground. Tyler and Nick were on the slide.

They lived next door to Posey. They were brothers.

"Hey, Posey!" they called.

Posey went over to them.

"Tyler and me want to make sure you're ready for first grade," Nick said.

"I'm getting new shoes," said Posey.

"You know you have to walk into the school by yourself, right?" said Tyler.

"I can do that," Posey said bravely.

"What about the hall?" asked Nick.

"What hall?" said Posey.

"The hall is long and dark," Tyler said in a spooky voice. He banged his foot on the slide.

Boom.

"You're all
by yourself."
Another
boom.

Posey looked up at him from the
bottom of the slide and shivered.

"If the monster grabs you, there's
no one around to help," said Nick.

"Monster?" said Posey. She looked from one boy to the other. "There's no monster at Middle Pond School."

"Oh, yes, there is," said Tyler. "Isn't there, Nick?"

He jabbed his younger brother in the side.

Nick nodded. "The Monster of the Blue Hall," he said.

The blue hall was for the first grade. Tyler was in the fourth grade. He was on the green hall.

Nick was on the red hall with the other second-graders.

"Most first-graders don't make it to their classrooms," Tyler said.

"The monster gets them first," said Nick. "It sucks out their blood. The rest get eaten by snakes."

"Snakes?" said Posey.

Nick and Tyler loved to tease her. They teased her all the time.

Posey knew they were teasing her now.

Still, she tightened her grip on her stuffed giraffe.

ONE WAY
TO
FIND OUT

"**I** never saw any snakes,"
said Posey.

"They don't come out for kinder-garteners," said Nick. "They only come out for first-graders."

"First-graders without their mothers," added Tyler.

Posey let out a little squeak. The boys fell against each other and laughed. They thought they were the smartest boys in the whole world.

It made Posey mad.

"How come the monster didn't get you?" she asked.

"It did," said Nick. "Didn't it, Tyler?"

Tyler nodded. "We don't have blood inside," he said.

"Everyone has blood," said Posey.

"Not Tyler and me," said Nick. "We have ink. Look."

The boys held out their wrists. Posey stared at their blue veins.

"Blood is red," Nick said in a spooky voice. "Ink is blue."

Posey knew Nick was trying to scare her. But what if what he said was true?

There was only one way to find out.

Posey picked up a stick and jabbed him.

NO SNAKES,
NO MONSTERS

Gramps came over to take Posey for a ride after dinner.

She was quiet when he pulled out of the driveway.

She was quiet when he tooted his horn two times to say good-bye to Danny.

"Cat got your tongue?" Gramps said. "You're mighty quiet tonight."

Posey shook her head. She didn't say a word.

"Your mom told me about Nick," Gramps said. "I guess you got him pretty good."

Posey stared out the window.

"Want to tell me about it?" Gramps asked.

Posey told him all about the Monster of the Blue Hall.

And the snakes.

And the first-graders
without their mothers.

The tight feeling in her chest
got looser as she talked. Gramps
reached over and patted her knee
when she was finished.

"They were pulling your leg, Posey," he said. "Blood looks blue until it hits the air. Then it's red. They were trying to scare you, that's all."

Posey looked at her arm. Her veins were blue, too. "There's no monster, is there, Gramps?" she said.

"Nope. No snakes, either. That school has been around since your mom was a little girl. No one has seen a monster yet."

It made Posey feel better to hear Gramps say it. But thinking about school still gave her a funny feeling in her stomach.

"What do you say we stop at Hank's and get an ice cream?" said Gramps.

He swung his truck into the dusty parking lot in front of a small store. He and Posey went inside.

"You go pick your flavor," said Gramps. "I want to pick up some milk."

Posey ran to the back of the store. She slid open the lid of the ice cream freezer. When she was too small to reach it, Gramps had to pull a wooden box over for her to stand on.

Now she stood on tiptoe and looked in. There were cherry, orange, and grape Popsicles. Posey picked cherry and slid the lid closed.

She started back to find Gramps.

Halfway down the aisle, Posey froze.

Miss Lee, her very own first-grade teacher, was standing at the front of the store. Posey saw her when she visited Miss Lee's class last year.

Seeing her in Hank's made Posey feel shy.

CHAPTER SIX

CHAPTER
SIX

A MOUSE
COULD HIDE

Posey wished she was a mouse so she could hide.

What if Miss Lee saw her? What if she talked to Posey and asked her questions?

"Posey," called a loud voice. "Over here!"

It was Gramps. He was in the line next to Miss Lee.

Posey ran and hid her face against his shirt. She felt his strong arm wrap around her.

"What's all this about?" said Gramps.

Before Posey could answer, she heard another voice.

"Hello, Posey."

Posey looked up.

Miss Lee was smiling at her.

"I'm Linda Lee," she told Gramps.

"Posey's first-grade teacher."

"What do you know about that, Posey?" said Gramps. "Your teacher shops at Hank's, too."

All Posey could do was nod.

CHAPTER SEVEN

POSEY'S
IDEA

"You'll like having Posey in your class," Gramps said. "She's a good girl and a hard worker."

"I'm sure she is," said Miss Lee. "I love your tutu, Posey. I love pink, too."

Miss Lee held out her foot. She was wearing pink sneakers. They looked like they had been washed a million times.

Her pinkie toe poked out through a hole in the end.

"These old things are ready for the trash," said Miss Lee. "But I can't bear to part with them."

"Posey is the same way," said Gramps. "She would wear her ballet outfit to school every day of the year, if she could."

"I know exactly how she feels."

Miss Lee squatted down so she could look into Posey's eyes. "I bet your tutu is comfortable, isn't it?" she said.

Posey nodded.

"My shoes are, too," said Miss Lee. "It's too bad we can't wear our favorite old clothes to school, isn't it?"

Posey stared back at her, round-eyed. "Why can't we?" she asked.

"Why can't we?" Miss Lee sounded surprised.

"Why can't everyone wear what they want to school?" Posey said bravely.

Miss Lee stood up. She squeezed her lips together and thought.

"Well, I guess because then we'd have pirates and clowns and super-heroes and ballet dancers in our class," she said at last.

"What's wrong with that?" said Posey.

"Now, Posey . . ." said Gramps.

"It's all right," Miss Lee told him. She smiled at Posey again.

Posey thought Miss Lee was pretty.

"That doesn't sound very much

like a first-grade class, does it?" said
Miss Lee.

"No," said Posey. "It sounds like
a parade."

CHAPTER
EIGHT

THE
MAGIC VEIL

Posey couldn't sit still. The invitation had come in the morning mail.

It was for Miss Lee's "First Day of First Grade Parade."

Dear First-Graders,

My friend Posey gave me a great idea yesterday. Because you are all so different and creative, you are invited to come to school dressed in your favorite clothes. We will have a parade to start off the new school year.

WHEN: The first day of school
WHERE: Middle Pond School, front steps
TIME: 8:00 a.m.

I will be outside to greet you. We will parade down the blue hall to our class.

Sincerely,
Miss Lee

Posey's tutu was clean and almost like new. Her mom had mended the hole and the tear.

Now Gramps was coming over to give Posey a present. She bounced up and down on the couch. She ran to the window to look out.

"He's here!" she shouted when Gramps's truck pulled into the driveway. She ran outside and hugged Gramps as hard as she could.

"Hang on now." Gramps laughed. "What's all the excitement?"

Posey's mom came out onto the front porch holding Danny. "Let

58

Gramps get inside," she called.

In the living room, Gramps handed Posey a shiny box with a silver bow.

"Go on, open it," he said.

Inside was a beautiful pink veil covered with stars. Posey held it up.

The stars sparkled like magic. They were blue and green and red.

"Put it on," said Gramps. "Let's see how it looks."

The veil fell around Posey's shoulders like a cloud.

A sparkly pink cloud.

Posey started to twirl. She twirled and twirled as if she would never stop.

"Posey, slow down," said her mom.

But Posey couldn't slow down. She was Princess Posey, the Pink Princess. Princess Posey was

floating.

Around and
around and around
like a dream.

When Posey bumped into the couch, Gramps put his arms around her.

"You know what makes that veil so magic?" he said.

"What?"

"You and that brave heart of yours. It's all you will ever need."

Posey knew Gramps was right.

CHAPTER NINE

POOR DANNY

"Poor Danny," Posey said as she got into bed. "He can't go to first grade tomorrow."

She curled up on her side so she could look at her veil. It was hanging on the back of her chair.

"How about a book?" said her mom.

"Not tonight," said Posey. "I want to fall asleep fast so it's tomorrow."

Her mom sat on the edge of Posey's bed.

"Now, remember," she said. "Tomorrow I'm going to stop the car at the Kiss and Go sign."

Posey nodded.

"You'll give me a kiss and walk up to the school, okay?"

"Miss Lee will be waiting," said Posey.

"Right."

"Miss Lee smiles a lot," Posey said sleepily.

"I'm glad," said her mom.

Her mom kissed her good night and turned off the light. But Posey didn't close her eyes.

She wanted to see if her veil sparkled in the dark.

It did.

With every new breeze that came through

the window, the stars twinkled in the light of the moon.

Right up to the minute Posey fell asleep.

Right on through the night.

They were twinkling in the sun the next morning when she opened her eyes.

It was the first day of first grade.

TICKLED PINK

The line of cars inched forward.

"Hurry, Mom, hurry!" Posey begged. She could hardly wait to reach the Kiss and Go Lane sign.

The minute they did, she opened her door.

"How about a kiss?" said her mom.

Posey gave her a kiss and got out of the car. There were children everywhere. Posey saw a cowboy. Then Miss Lee's smiling face.

"How about Danny?" her mom called.

"Bye-bye, Danny!" Posey cried. She blew him a kiss and ran toward Miss Lee.

Miss Lee was surrounded by children. They didn't look like

they were dressed for school at all!
Posey saw a girl in her pajamas and
a boy in a soccer uniform. Another
boy wore huge dinosaur slippers.

There was even a girl wearing a
tutu.

Her tutu was blue.

"I wish I had a veil with sparkles,"
she said.

Miss Lee put her hands on Posey's shoulders.

"All right, everyone," she called. "I want you all to line up behind Posey."

Everyone rushed to get in line. The cowboy was first behind Posey. Then the girl in the blue tutu. She had curly blond hair.

She smiled at Posey.

Posey smiled back.

The line was wiggling and squirming like a worm. Miss Lee held up her hand.

"Listen carefully," she said. "We are going to march into the school and down the blue hall to our room. Is everybody ready?"

"READY!" shouted the worm.

"Follow Posey," said Miss Lee. "She's the leader today."

So Miss Lee's class paraded through the school. The other children stood and clapped.

Miss Lee's children smiled and smiled. But the biggest smile was at the head of the line. It was Princess Posey, and she was tickled pink.

P🌸SEY'S PAGES

Posey loves making friends
and learning more about new
people. Here are some
questions she'd ask you
if she could:

My first grade parade was so much fun!
What would you wear if your
class had a first grade parade?

I have a stuffed giraffe named Roger. He's white with blue spots. He sleeps with me every night. Do you have a favorite stuffed animal? What is its name? What does it look like?

• • •

I was nervous about starting first grade. Were you? What were you scared about? If you're in kindergarten, how do you feel about first grade?

• • •

I feel special when I wear my pink tutu, like a brave princess. Do you have something you wear that makes you feel special? What is it? How does it make you feel?

• • •

Someday, I want to ride the bus to school with my friends. Do you ride the bus? Is it fun?

• • •

I felt shy when I saw Miss Lee in Hank's store. I wanted to hide. Have you ever seen your teacher outside of school? What did you do?

• • •

Making friends at school is so much fun. Who are some of the friends you've made? What do you like to do together?

• • •

Nick and Tyler tease me a lot. They scared me about the Monster of the Blue Hall. Does anyone you know tease you? What do they tease you about? What do you do?

STEPHANIE GREENE is the author of the popular Owen Foote, Sophie Hartley, and Moose and Hildy series. Over the years, she has spotted pink, purple, green, and blue princesses everywhere she goes: in libraries, at schools, in airports, and on city streets. She's delighted to introduce them all to Posey, and hopes they will become fast friends. Stephanie Greene lives in Chapel Hill, North Carolina. Visit her online at www.stephaniegreenebooks.com.

STEPHANIE ROTH SISSON illustrates picture books and chapter books, including the Bitty Twins series. Her work has been called "delightfully expressive" and "affectionate." She remembers the fear of starting first grade and wishes she had a tutu and a teacher like Miss Lee. Stephanie Roth Sisson lives in Shell Beach, California. Visit her online at www.stephanitely.com.